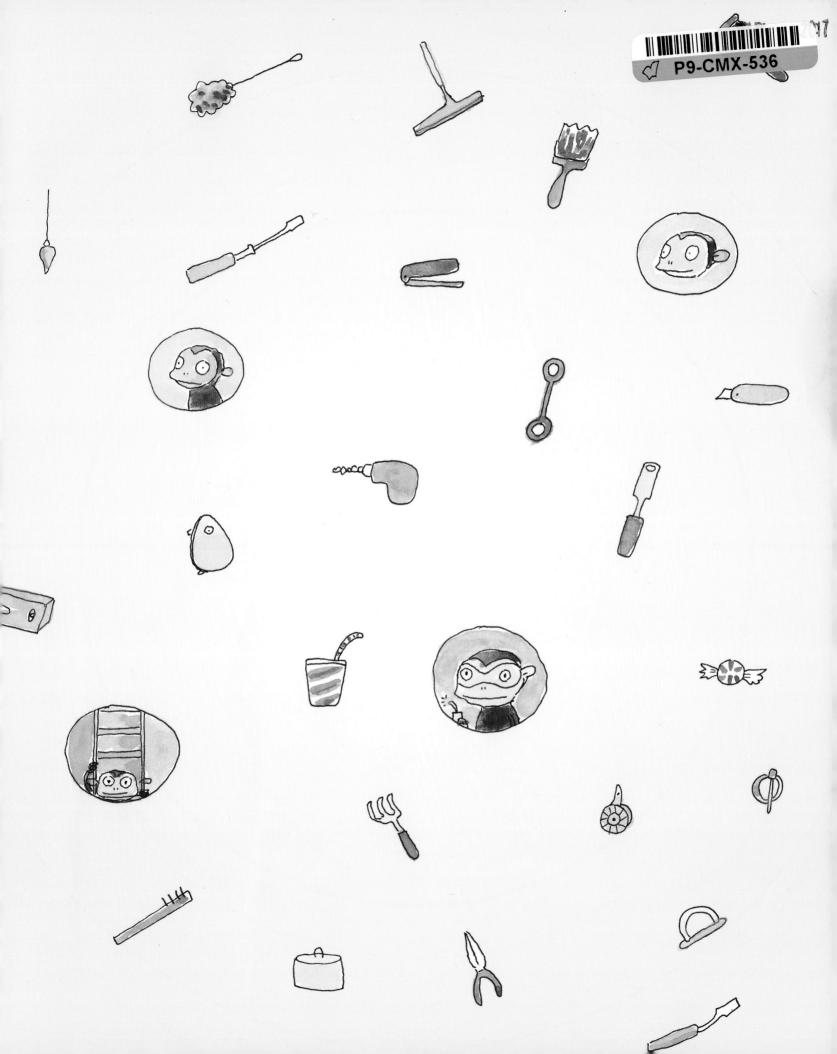

Monkey With A Tool Belt

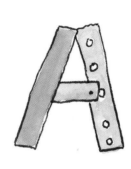

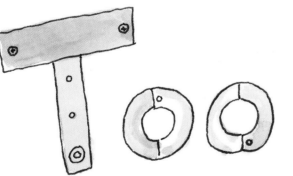

Chris Monroe

CAROLRHODA BOOKS MINNEAPOLIS

For my parents — CM

Copyright © 2008 by Chris Monroe

Carolrhoda Books
A division of Lerner Publishing Group, Inc.
241 First Avenue North
Minneapolis, MN 55401 USA

For reading levels and more information, look up this title at www.lernerbooks.com.

Library of Congress Cataloging-in-Publication Data

Monroe, Chris.
    Monkey with a tool belt / by Chris Monroe.
        p.   cm.
    Summary: Clever monkey Chico Bon Bon builds lots of things with his many tools, and when he is captured by an organ-grinder, he uses them to help him escape and get back home.
    ISBN: 978-0-8225-7631-0 (lib. bdg. : alk. paper)
    ISBN: 978-0-7613-3971-7 (EB pdf)
    [1. Tools—Fiction. 2. Building—Fiction. 3. Monkeys—Fiction. 4. Animals—Fiction.] 1. Title.
PZ7.M76OMo 2008
    [E]—dc22   2007010020

Manufactured in the United States of America
8-43132-8548-11/1/2016

Here is **Chico Bon Bon**.

He is a monkey.

Chico is a monkey with a **tool belt**.

He is quite handy
with tools.

He **builds** and **fixes**
all sorts of things.

some of Chico's tools

screwdriver
nut driver
nutcracker
squeegee
ouija
planer
strainer
grease container
bungee hammer
scrunchy hammer
monkey wrench
turkey wrench
donkey wrench

drill
drill bits
zoozle
zoozle bits

bottle brush

lifter
puller
claw hammer
tack hammer
pajama hammer
banana hammer
clam hammer
stapler
staple remover
shozzer
shozz remover
needle nose
greaser
tweezer
lemon squeezer

All his tools fit on his **belt**.

Every day, Chico builds or fixes something
for his friends and his family.

He is very **creative**.

He builds a dock for
the ducks

cutters

and a clock for
the Clucks.

twist-it

He uses his nippers for
nipping and tucks.

nippers

He uses his level on a toy
box for Neville.

TOYS

level

bevel

wongler

Wood wonglers are needed to
make this nice bevel.

He builds a go-kart for Go-Go to transport the skunks

wrench

and a small roller coaster for local chipmunks.

screwdriver

Pipeline!

awesome tool belt

sweet!

He'll need all his drill bits to fix up this ramp,

dude

totally

plus a chisel, a frizzle, and a giant C-clamp.

drill bits

chisel

frizzle

c-clamp

Sometimes he makes a mistake . . .

. . . but he just finds the
right tool and fixes it.

One day, Chico noticed a **banana split** on a tiny
table across the road from his house.

He went over to investigate.

Chico tasted the mysterious banana split.
It was fake! He wondered why a banana split would
be made of plastic.

Just then, a big box came down on top of him.

It was a trap!

He was **captured!**

He looked out of a hole in the box and
saw an organ-grinder from the circus.

This organ-grinder needed a new monkey. His old monkey, Bobo, had run away earlier that week with the help of several circus tigers.

Chico could not get out.

The organ-grinder locked the box
and bungeed it to his bicycle.

He rode a long, long way.

It was a rough ride.

Chico felt lucky the banana split wasn't real. He would have been covered in ice cream.

The organ-grinder rode all the way to the
circus camp on the other side of town.

He carried the box inside his trailer. He began to make dinner.

He used an egg beater, a blender, a can opener, a vacuum cleaner, and a coffee grinder. It was all extremely noisy.

Chico watched him through the hole in the box. The man didn't realize that Chico was wearing his tool belt.

Chico had a plan:

1. He stuck his measuring tape through the hole.

He measured the distance to the door.

2. He measured the hole.

3. He wrote down the numbers with his pencil and divided by 47.

4. He put a bendy extender with a rearview mirror attachment on his drill.

It just barely fit through the hole.

5. He loosened the screws on the box lid with the drill.

6. He double-checked the organ-grinder.

7 He used a mini file to make the hole bigger.

8 He made the hole even bigger with a tiny hacksaw, a hole razzer, a half-inch beebersaw, a small jimmy-jubber, and some sandpaper.

9 He sliced the plastic banana split with his utility-knife-lemon-squeezer-flashlight-banana-peeler.

(It's one of the best multi-use tools around.)

10 He disguised the hole with sawdust, spackle, and a piece of the plastic banana split.

11 Then he made a loud water-buffalo noise with his kazoo.

UHWOOGAA

12 The organ-grinder looked over.

What?

whirrrr

He walked over to the box . . . .

Suddenly, Chico used his rubber hammer
on the man's big toe!

The man leaped back on one foot,

holding his big toe and hopping about!

Chico pushed open the box lid and jumped out.

He ran out the door.

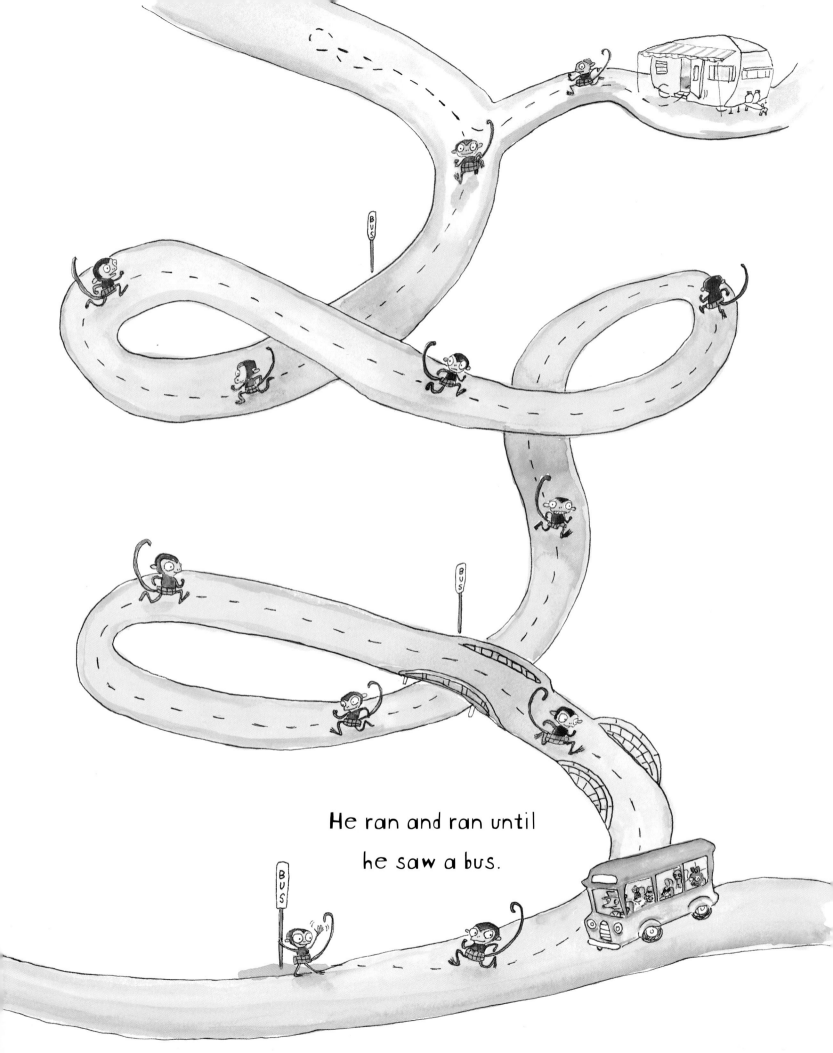

He ran and ran until
he saw a bus.

He fished some change
out of his tool belt

and got on the bus.

He rode the bus to his house.

Chico was home!

"Good thing **I** have this tool belt," Chico Bon Bon said to himself. He took the tool belt off and laid it on his dresser.

He put on his pajamas.

Then he put his tool belt back on and climbed into bed.

Well, good night, Chico Bon Bon!

I wonder what he'll build tomorrow?